The Tooth Fairy

Written by Kirsten Hall
Illustrated by Dawn Apperley

My First
READER

SCHOLASTIC INC.

New York   Toronto   London   Auckland   Sydney
Mexico City   New Delhi   Hong Kong   Buenos Aires

ISBN 0-516-24801-4

12 11 10 9 8 7 6 5 4 3 2 1   4 5 6 7 8 9/0

Printed in the U.S.A.   61

First Scholastic paperback printing, February 2004

Note to Parents and Teachers

Once a reader can recognize and identify the 34 words
used to tell this story, he or she will be able to read successfully
the entire book. These 34 words are repeated throughout the story,
so that young readers will be able to easily recognize
the words and understand their meaning.

The 34 words used in this book are:

be	here	open	tight
bed	I'll	out	time
close	it	pass	to
clouds	it's	she'll	tonight
come	keep	soon	tooth
eyes	look	stars	up
fairy	moon	surprises	will
fell	my	the	
go	near	them	

My tooth fell out.

Look here!

Look here!

I'll go to bed.

I'll keep it near.

I'll close my eyes.

I'll close them tight!

The tooth fairy
will come tonight.

She'll pass the stars.

She'll pass the moon.

She'll pass the clouds.

She'll be here soon.

It's time to open up my eyes!

It's time to open my surprise!

ABOUT THE AUTHOR

Kirsten Hall has lived most of her life in New York City. While she was still in high school, she published her first book for children, *Bunny, Bunny*. Since then, she has written and published more than sixty children's books. A former early education teacher, Kirsten currently works as a children's book editor.

ABOUT THE ILLUSTRATOR

Dawn Apperley studied graphic design in college and began illustrating children's books as soon as she graduated. Born in England, she has lived in the United States and Spain. Apperley enjoys cycling, inline skating, and gardening. She currently lives in London with her small white rabbit, Coco.